# The Cats
## Of Hanover Juvenile Correctional Center

Teresa Adele Bettino

Tate Publishing & *Enterprises*

"The Cats of Hanover Juvenile Correctional Center" by Teresa Adele Bettino

Copyright © 2006 by Teresa Adele Bettino. All rights reserved.

Published in the United States of America
by Tate Publishing, LLC
127 East Trade Center Terrace
Mustang, OK 73064
(888) 361-9473

Book design copyright © 2006 by Tate Publishing, LLC. All rights reserved.

No part of this publication may be reproduced, stored in a retrieval system or transmitted in any way by any means, electronic, mechanical, photocopy, recording or otherwise without the prior permission of the author except as provided by USA copyright law.

Scripture quotations marked "TLB" are taken from The Living Bible / Kenneth N. Taylor: Tyndale House, © Copyright 1997, 1971 by Tyndale House Publishers, Inc Used by permission. All rights reserved.

The opinions expressed by the author are not necessarily those of Tate Publishing, LLC.

This novel is a work of fiction. However, the Preface and Epilogue denote the accounts of what transpired at Hanover Juvenile Correctional Center. The story itself is a work of fiction. Names, characters, and incidents either are a product of the author's imagination, or are used fictitiously. Any resemblance to actual persons, living or dead, and events at Hanover Juvenile Correctional Center or locales is entirely coincidental.

ISBN: 1-5988647-9-3

060606

# Dedication

In memory of the cats of Hanover Juvenile Correctional Center. I miss each one of you.

Warm memories of my grandmothers, Adele Gondolfo and Anna Mumola, who Momma Mola is named after. Special memories of Cathy Cheek, who was instrumental in adopting and loving many of Hanover's cats, especially Miss Tina.

I would like to thank those individuals who attempted to save this colony: Tina Hughes, Don Driscoll, and Hanover Humane.

Proofreaders: Jean Rollins, Susan Saathoff, Carol Young, and Fran Kinneberg. Thanks for your guidance and diligence.

"Civilization is a stream with banks. The stream is sometimes filled with blood from people killing, stealing, shouting and doing things the historians usually record, while on the banks, unnoticed, people build homes, make love, raise children, sing songs, write poetry and even whittle statues. The story of civilization is what happened on the banks."
-Will Durant, *Civilization*

# Preface

Turning down the long, hilly road leading to the correctional center, I drive slowly looking for deer and signs of wildlife. Since 1997, the correctional officer at the security shed greets me, wanting to know how the cats are. What am I to say? The feral cat program called Hanover Trap-Neuter-Return Program is no longer.

The Hanover Juvenile Correctional Center's Trap-Neuter-Return Program began with two individuals who were employed at the institution in 1997. Teresa Adele Bettino and Tina Hughes were instrumental with addressing the feline overpopulation problem that plagued the correctional center. Thanks to the blessing of the animal friendly superintendent, the program commenced with the understanding that feral cats had the right to live peacefully on State land.

Since 1997, over forty cats left the center and were adopted.

Majestic as the free-roaming ponies of Chincoteague, Virginia, the feral cats of Hanover Juvenile Correctional Center were a tradition. Generations of beautiful feral cats had been seen wandering the 1800 acres for many years and did not harm anyone. However, a current superintendent thought otherwise, and an established neutered colony of six to eight cats was destroyed. The cats were blamed for scratching vehicles, as well as for a raccoon population that had set up housekeeping on the premises during the summer of 2004.

As I continue to work through the many layers of government bureaucracy and resistance, I take a deep breath and ponder how individuals within Virginia's government can get away with this behavior. I continue to pray to St. Francis for the souls of these animals and pray that the superintendent will take ownership for her actions, as euthanasia is not the answer.

Issues relating to the care of feral cats are a national problem and need to be recognized. A trap-neuter-return program works, if given the opportunity.

# Table of Contents

The Old Lady Who Lived In A Shoe . . . . . . . . . . . . . . . 11
Political Correctness, A Must For Any Feline . . . . . . . . 15
Barefoot And Pregnant Again . . . . . . . . . . . . . . . . . . . . 19
Humans Dumping Cats . . . . . . . . . . . . . . . . . . . . . . . . . 25
The Midnight Express . . . . . . . . . . . . . . . . . . . . . . . . . . 29
Catnip And Other Herbs. . . . . . . . . . . . . . . . . . . . . . . . 35
Cat On a Hot Tin Roof. . . . . . . . . . . . . . . . . . . . . . . . . . 39
Miss Tina's Second Life. . . . . . . . . . . . . . . . . . . . . . . . 45
The Famous Mister Ed. . . . . . . . . . . . . . . . . . . . . . . . . 49
The Cat's Out Of The Bag . . . . . . . . . . . . . . . . . . . . . . 53
The Dog Days Of Summer . . . . . . . . . . . . . . . . . . . . . . 57
My Cat's Meow . . . . . . . . . . . . . . . . . . . . . . . . . . . . . . . 61
Barking Up The Wrong Tree . . . . . . . . . . . . . . . . . . . . 65
Momma's New Home . . . . . . . . . . . . . . . . . . . . . . . . . . 69
The Empty Cat Syndrome . . . . . . . . . . . . . . . . . . . . . . 73
Pumpkin's Ninth Life. . . . . . . . . . . . . . . . . . . . . . . . . . 77
Epilogue. . . . . . . . . . . . . . . . . . . . . . . . . . . . . . . . . . . . 80
Bibliography . . . . . . . . . . . . . . . . . . . . . . . . . . . . . . . . 82

# Chapter 1
## The Old Lady Who Lived In a Shoe

I have never understood how I became known as Momma Mola. Some say it is because in my heyday, I was like the "Old Lady Who Lived in A Shoe," I had so many kittens that I just did not know what to do! I was the top-of-the-line, blue-blooded feline that happened to make my residence on the campus of Hanover Juvenile Correctional Center. As a female, non-neutered cat, I was the envy of those straggly cats at the nearby landfill, known as "dump cats."

Hanover Juvenile Correctional Center, a juvenile prison with a population of two hundred inmates, or teenagers, was the place to live for any feline residing in the county. The boys, as I fondly called them, loved to feed me. The dining hall had good food, especially on Fridays, when the cook baked fish. Another good night to hang around campus was fried chicken night, which was better than any of the popular fast food chains or local grocery stores. It was toe-licking good!

In the spring, when the grass started to become green and the days became longer, I would enjoy snoozing in the sun by the pond. The pond offered drinking water and fresh fish. It also offered field mice and birds. At times, Canadian geese would come and spend a few days, although I did not waste my time hunting a goose. The geese were too large and time-consuming to eat for my taste. I liked to have a quick dinner, which was offered in dumpsters and by the dining hall chef.

What a wonderful place to live. Free food, free water, and lots of attention from free-roaming Toms.

Those roaming Toms would try to smooth talk me, and would take me out on dates. The dates were usually a walk over to the dining hall where the cook would leave tidbits by the dumpster.

I remember one big fat Tom named Charlie Brown, and as the song goes, "He was a clown, that Charlie Brown." He would clean himself and grease the fur on his head to hide his bald spot. With every ounce of energy, he would strut his stuff over to the center from the nearby cattle farm. To me, he always smelled of stale cow manure mixed with dried mud and drool.

What the heck, when you need a date, you will take almost anything that comes down the beaten path, and although Charlie was not known as a big spender, he would at least pick a flower from the nearby field and hand it to me when we would meet.

Our meeting place was a large bush that bloomed beautiful red flowers in the spring, near the woods and close to the administration building. Charlie always had one thing on his mind, and he would always try to get me in the mood for a little romancing, especially when I was catnapping under the red bush.

When Charlie heard music from the boys' boom boxes, he would find some extra energy and start to hip-hop to the beat. Charlie would "find his groove" and let loose. But with a large belly and short skinny legs, the beat was lost and all the grooving took its toll on poor Charlie's back.

I recall one of Charlie's big moves was to take me in his arms, spin me around, and hold me with his front legs. He would attempt to engage me, but due to his fish breath, I would quickly move my face away and break from his hold. At times, Charlie would lift his tail and stand on his two front legs, throwing his back legs up and out. What a sight for my cat eyes! Charlie would try to maneuver me to one of the State cars sitting idly in the parking lot. He hoped that the back window was open so we could jump in for a ride.

However, one fault amongst his many was that Charlie didn't particularly like humans.

"Black cats don't like humans," he used to say.

He stayed away from humans. I used to think, *my oh my, how cats can be prejudiced. There is nothing wrong with humans. They give me tidbits of food, and the cook leaves me the catch of the day on Fridays.*

Unfortunately, Charlie Brown fathered six of my kittens, and some had his personality.

## Chapter 2
## Political Correctness, a Must for Any Feline

The humans in charge of the center were interesting. You see, being a free-roaming feline can take some political maneuvering at times. Superintendents are transferred to other facilities, and depending on what side of the fence you're sitting on, as a cat you are loved by the human in charge and sometimes not.

So, Momma, as I was fondly called, needed to know who was in charge and which way those in charge swayed.

One superintendent I remember, named Donald, was a caring man who enjoyed animals living on campus. An old hunting dog named Sally once came to the center during hunting season, and since no one claimed her, Donald had old Sally fixed so that she would not be able to have pups.

Sally lived on campus and spent the rest of her days being cared for by the maintenance crew. Sally had the life of leisure. She was the "queen bee," high enough on the pecking order to get to sit in the golf cart and be chauffeured around all day. She was even allowed to go into the administration building when the maintenance men were repairing broken plumbing.

The boys especially loved Sally as she played fetch and swam in the pool with them during the summer. Luckily, for Sally, the cook liked her and would save steak bones.

Sally enjoyed Founder's Day when parents would come to visit their children. The center would have lots of food, and Sally especially enjoyed eating barbeque ribs.

I often wondered how I could get a high rank like Sally, although I always thought that cats were higher on the social scale than dogs. Gosh, how could anyone like dogs? They have an offensive odor when wet. They shake, getting the wet and the smell on anyone within one foot of them.

A cat, on the other hand, really doesn't like to get wet, and will groom to perfection until no odor is found. I must say that we are particular as to where we use the bathroom. I once witnessed Sally having a bowel movement under the State flag in front of Donald and the Director of the Department, who also happened to be a local minister. They attempted to ignore the sight; however, they were downwind to the odor!

How politically correct was that? I would never do anything like that. To Sally's credit, she was the most pampered animal on campus, and I must say we did have a lot of animals on campus.

## Chapter 3
## Barefoot and Pregnant Again

Charlie impregnated me on an unusually warm spring evening when the moon was full and the boom boxes were earsplitting. The rap music got Charlie's juices flowing, and I let down my guard. The back window of a State bus had been left open, we jumped in, and the next thing I knew, old Charlie was gone and I was pregnant.

I was stuck raising six children. I never saw Charlie again. I heard through the grapevine that a cow from the nearby cattle farm had kicked him in the head, and instead of the "cow that jumped over the moon," Charlie flew over it and was never seen again. I didn't mind because he had a negative attitude about humans.

Luckily, as my weight increased, Terry, who worked at the center and cared for us, noticed my body changing. Terry began to feed me a little more and to spend some extra time with me. On nights that she facilitated an anger control group with the boys, she would eat dinner in the dining hall and save good quality tidbits for me.

I often questioned if the anger control group worked. There were a lot of anger control issues at Hanover. Sometimes, I think the boys had less anger control issues than the correctional officers and administrators in charge of the facility.

I would hear of boys graduating from the group, only to find themselves in trouble for hitting another boy the next day. At times, I had to move quickly around campus in order to miss being in the line of fire. When I saw a boy with a mischievous sparkle in his eye and a little smirk to his mouth, I knew to move quickly because a swift kick might be coming my way.

Some correctional officers had bad attitudes and poor self-control. They were in need of anger management groups. The officers described one who had an attitude problem as "havin' a bad 'tude!" After a stressful shift or being angry with a co-worker, it was not unusual for an officer to take his keys and walk along side a chosen car, scratching it. Many times, it was a brand new Lexus. What a mess that would be when the owner of the Lexus noticed the scratch marks. Suddenly, the cats were at fault. The cats caused the scratches with their claws.

When I gave birth to my kittens, Terry found them and made sure that predators did not harm my babies. I had made my home in a thicket where I was able to have privacy and protection near a building called the Smokehouse. This building was no longer in use and made a good shelter. The thicket kept my babies sheltered from rain, wind, and predators.

When my babies were old enough for some socialization, I carried them, one by one, to the administration building in order to show them to my friend. Terry came quickly out of her office, down the steps, and eagerly congratulated me. Terry proceeded to name my brood.

The all black kitten that resembled Charlie Brown was the firstborn. Terry named him Midnight, as he was as black as night. From the beginning, he was friendly and loved excitement. He was audacious and enjoyed playing with his siblings.

My second born, a calico, who resembled me, was named Miss Tina, after a co-worker. Miss Tina was quiet and enjoyed watching situations unfold. The co-worker loved taking care of us. Many a day I heard Tina say, "I come to work for these cats, that's the only reason. This place will drive you nuts!"

Terry, a horse-lover, named my third born after the famous horse, Mister Ed. She said that my baby had the head and teeth similar to a horse, and snorted like one, too. Mr. Ed was as cantankerous as the horse on the television series. My son was opinionated and domineering. He also was easily swayed by his siblings' thoughts and actions. One minute he would side with Miss Tina, and the next minute he would be on the side of Midnight. Mister Ed, from his early beginnings, had a way of browbeating his siblings into submission. He sat on the fence a lot and waited to decide what action to take.

The fourth baby, a male with black and white spots and very short chicken legs, was called Julian. He was a needy baby, always droning. His humming was so repetitious that his other siblings used to swat at him with ears pinned. Another trait he possessed was utter slothfulness. He was late for feedings, slow to clean, and when matured, loved trashy female felines. He loved to wander to the nearby sanitation dump. Terry nicknamed him Player since he had a lust for trashy women.

My fifth kitten was named Pumpkin Face, whose face resembled a jack-o-lantern. Pumpkin had a face only his mother could and would love. He had a large triangle over his nose that made him look silly. However, he was the most thoughtful and kindest of my children. Pumpkin enjoyed time spent with me, and especially enjoyed sunning himself near the pond on a warm day. He loved to dip his paws into the water as he lay by the side of the pond. He was the sunshine of my life and stayed close to my side.

The last-born was a tubby runt. Terry said that this kitten reminded her of a sordid administrator. Terry named her Ms. Heavens, as she felt that my baby was in need of saintly graces. From the earliest beginnings as she nursed, Ms. Heavens pushed her way amongst her siblings to reach me first. She nursed with great enthusiasm. As she grew fatter by the day, she found great liking in attempting to boss her siblings. She especially enjoyed bossing Julian around. Terry labeled her a "micromanager," as she was always pointing her paw in various directions giving orders to Julian, who lacked chutzpah, or self-confidence.

The gene pool is an amazing occurrence as Julian, Ms. Heavens, and Mister Ed took after Charlie Brown. Having the three of them within one litter put a strain on my mental well-being. However, Miss Tina, Midnight, and Pumpkin Face had my wonderful personality, and were a delight to parent.

Hanover County
Trash Collection

## Chapter 4
### Humans Dumping Cats

Times were trying at Hanover Juvenile Correctional Center as my kittens matured. Humans were dumping off their cats on campus and at the local dump not far up the road. Cats were roaming the campus at night, getting food from dumpsters, and females were having litter after litter under sheds and outbuildings.

Terry worked hard with trapping feral cats and finding homes for us. Felines who could be adopted were given to responsible humans. Those that couldn't be adopted; she neutered and returned to the center. Terry made the feline population at the center manageable; however, humans continued to abandon their cats. Kittens, pregnant cats, and Toms were dumped. These cats were confused, sometimes sick, wandering around the vast acreage in search of food and shelter. Some cried throughout the long nights, in search for the human who had taken care of them.

When I think about it, something similar to this happened to me. I can remember having a family. I can remember my family moving their possessions out of the house and placing me on the porch with no food or water. When my family didn't return by nightfall, I was confused. I had no food, water, or my familiar litter pan. I remember saying, "meow, meow," throughout the night, but no one opened the back door or switched on the back porch light. What had happened to my family?

My stomach hungry and my tongue parched, I realized my situation. I began to roam and walked up River Road until I came to a cattle farm. I could smell water and food. I decided to take up residence at the center, because there were many outbuildings that would provide shelter. I missed my family. Why had they left? Why had they not taken me?

One time, I spotted a correctional officer dropping off a domestic, longhaired, silvery gray pregnant cat. The poor cat did not know how to fend for herself. She meowed throughout the first night, and when it began to rain, she did not know where to go to get out of the elements. Luckily, for this cat, my friend Terry picked her up and took her inside the administration building. The next thing I heard was that Terry had contacted someone from Hanover Humane. The pregnant cat was placed in a safe house. I think that this was best for this poor cat. She had not been raised feral and had not developed survival skills.

Living a free-roaming life is not a picnic. It takes much resourcefulness, as any feral cat will tell you.

## Chapter 5
## The Midnight Express

My six babies grew into teenagers quickly and Terry was able to trap, neuter, and return them to the center. The personality conflicts within our family nearly drove me to drink.

My curious one, Midnight, enjoyed exploring the center grounds at night. He did this after correctional officers had tucked the boys into bed. He could be seen climbing the fence, which kept the boys in and us out. Due to the blackness of his fur, he strolled around campus undetected. At times, he would eavesdrop on staff conversations. Midnight loved excitement and loved to gossip.

He once told me about female and male officers making dates to meet on break, and especially enjoyed spying on officers in compromising positions. One time he told the tale of two counselors who were enjoying their private office on campus, away from their supervisor and the boys. He had climbed to the second floor and watched from the windowsill. I would admonish Midnight for being curious, as his curiosity almost caused his demise the night of the great escape.

I scolded Midnight for traveling onto campus. I was concerned that he would befriend one of the boys. I knew that the boys had their share of problems, or else they would not have been locked up in the interest of public safety. So I tried hard to place limits on the amount of time Midnight roamed at night unsupervised. I did not want my son influenced.

I remember the night Midnight went on a joy ride with two of the boys. These boys were housed in Winston Cottage, the maximum-security building. One boy, a long-haired hippie type, and another, a blond-haired, blue-eyed country boy, had their minds set to escape. All doors were supposed to be secured, and the play yard had a large high fence surrounding it. Taxpayers' monies had been used to design this escape-proof cottage.

One night, after the correctional officers had completed a head count of their charges, they settled down to a quiet midnight shift. While the officers were dreaming in the wee early morning, these two became energetic and ambitious. They stuffed their cots with clothing and whittled their way out of their cells by manipulating the locks on their doors. With the synchronized snoring of the officers, the whittling was unheard. The opening of doors was not discovered, and the boys escaped over the razor-wired fence, through the woods and out into a sleeping rural community.

Midnight, snooping and lurking around campus, heard the commotion. He abandoned his search of rodents in order to have some fun. Upon hearing the uproar, he decided to investigate. With his lean, black, muscular body, he crawled behind the boys. He followed them around campus and watched as they shimmied their way through the razor wire on top of the fence. He watched as they jumped down and rolled onto the grass. Midnight followed, squeezing through the bottom of the fence, and ran with the boys.

They ran through cattle farm fields and across River Road. They soon discovered a Cape Cod home without the protection of lights. The foggy, early morning offered the boys and Midnight safety from discovery. A large Ford Explorer was in the driveway. At first, the boys thought to jimmy some wires, but the hippie opened the front door and noticed that the keys were in the ignition. He turned the ignition, and the country boy opened the car's back door.

Midnight was standing by the vehicle's back door trying to catch his breath, when the door opened and the country boy threw some clothing onto the backseat. While the door was open, Midnight jumped in.

The boys and Midnight were off and running. They traveled Interstate 64 East, heading for Virginia Beach.

At times during the drive, the boys weaved in and out of traffic, ran into a few convenience stores, stealing food and sodas, only to return to the vehicle and take off at high speeds. Midnight stayed in the back seat, feeling nauseous, and praying to Saint Jude for protection. He thought of his momma. He thought of his home. He thought that he had used one of his nine lives.

Midnight became alarmed when the boys began to argue; as when the country boy in the passenger seat grabbed the steering wheel, Midnight knew that he was in trouble. He wished that he had listened to his momma.

The car veered off the Interstate and landed in a marsh. Once the Explorer was stuck in the marsh, the boys opened the car doors. Still yelling at each other, they took off through the marsh, leaving the car doors open. With water coming onto the floor, Midnight escaped, doggy paddling out of the marsh and onto some high grassy area. He sat there amongst the mosquitoes until the sun rose, meowing for his momma.

As morning came and head counts commenced, things fell apart at the juvenile correctional center. While I was doing a head count for my six, the center realized that their head count was minus two inmates. Try as the guards might to get the population count correct, the count continued to be two short. My count was one short, and I quickly realized that Midnight was missing. By breakfast time, the superintendent and administrators were called to work. I roamed the center, searching frantically for my son.

As the owner of the Explorer, which had been stolen, peered out of his kitchen window while eating an energy bar, a Channel 6 news reporter was outside of Hanover Juvenile Correctional Center informing viewers of an escape. The energy bar fell onto the kitchen floor as he realized his vehicle was not in his driveway. He was heard yelling for his wife as he ran out the kitchen door.

Midnight returned to the center several weeks later, thinner, and with sores on his paws. He slept for three days under the red-flowering bush with his food and water supply close by. Terry pampered him, and I swatted him on his tail end. My friendly, audacious son would be in the doghouse for many days as he recuperated from his journey.

The boys were captured and transferred to another juvenile correctional center. The sleeping guards were fired.

The neighbor called his auto insurance company and lawyer. The Department of Juvenile Justice wrote a large check to him. Terry said, "Good fences make good neighbors!"

# Chapter 6
## Catnip and Other Herbs

Julian did not inherit my sense of work ethic. He was a lazy sort who would watch a mouse scurry as he lay sunning himself near the bank of the pond. He enjoyed loafing and having food handed to him by the volunteers who fed us. As he grew, his chicken legs tilted and bowed which caused him to sway his hips much as a pregnant woman.

Ms. Heavens, always the bossy-type, and always on the portly side, would waddle up to him and fall on her back and let Julian groom her to perfection. Ms Heavens and Julian had a symbiotic relationship, and try as I might, they were inseparable. Fat and a browbeater, Ms. Heavens loved to manipulate Julian, who had an inherent weakness for woman on the trashy side. Finding a comfortable spot close to food and the pond, he would groom his sister for hours on end.

Ms. Heavens had a fancy for tuna. At times, Terry would say she was "driven" for her tuna delight. No other food would do when she was in that mind frame, and luckily, for her, the chef baked or fried a large batch every other day. Her favorite type of tuna was marinated in garlic with a dash of oregano. A little squeeze of lemon over the tuna added a slight tartness to it. The tuna was scrumptious, and as it slowly cooked, the aroma would carry to the red-flowering bush where Julian was found sleeping off a meal, enjoying a catnap. It was not unusual for Ms. Heavens to drool and point a paw in the direction of the dining hall when she smelled the familiar aroma. When she smelled the whiff of tuna, she would move her paw, indicating the direction of the smell, and point to Julian.

Julian, so gnarly, coupled with his runt sister, reminded Terry of "the odd couple." As a teenager, Ms. Heavens continued to be generously proportioned, especially around the hindquarters, and kept herself groomed, whereas, Julian was dirty, smelly, and unkempt. When they were spotted walking together, they swayed conjoined.

On tuna days, Julian would be found along with Sally, the dog, begging for food on the loading dock of the dining hall. The chef would come out to greet them. The chef, a rather cheery large man, would talk to Julian and Sally simultaneously. Julian would rub his body along the side of the chef's legs, while Sally would throw her head high and yowl. He would give Julian some morsels of tuna by placing the tuna on a paper plate. Julian would carry the plate of tuna to where his sister waited. Sally would gobble her food in one breath and after finishing, would throw her head high, and yowl again, wanting more.

Although the smell of tuna in the air was fancied by us, on some nights the air was filled with a pleasant, one-of-a-kind smell. The smell seemed to come from a cottage named Crump. Terry told me that Crump Cottage was a cottage for boys who were incarcerated for committing crimes due to substance abuse addiction. I never really understood what she meant by that.

Since I followed Terry around campus and mimicked her breathing, I would suddenly feel relaxed, and later hungry. Any food would do, especially something sweet, and sweet to me was milk, cow's milk! With the cattle farm next door and lots of momma cows available, there was a generous supply of cow's milk. With a little milk in my stomach and a roll in some wild catnip, I was good for the night. What a wonderful life my children and I had living at the center. Life in the fast lane.

# Chapter 7
## Cat on a Hot Tin Roof

Cats are inquisitive by nature, and Miss Tina was analytical and enjoyed surveillance. She found pleasure from watching humans coming and going from the center. She was not an impulsive cat, though, and thought through situations. The goings-on of the center intrigued her.

When school started in September, the boys formed lines and marched into school. One day, Miss Tina decided to march with the JROTC cadets into the classroom. No one saw Miss Tina since she blended with the BDU, or Battle Dress Uniform. These were uniforms worn by boys in the JROTC program. They were shades of brown and green, known as camouflage. Since Miss Tina, a brown and black shorthaired calico, blended with the cadets and the surrounding woods, she was able to make herself invisible.

With the posture of a soldier marching, Miss Tina strutted into school, keeping the marching beat. The boys said, "Column right," and Miss Tina moved right. When the boys said, "Count off 1-2, 3-4," Miss Tina was on the mark and moved with the fourth boy.

She scampered into math class and positioned herself under the desk of a student, who was not the brightest. This student had not learned how to add, subtract, multiply, or divide, and was age thirteen. Miss Tina had heard the teachers talking about this boy and said, "He's from

Southwest Virginia, back in the hills, if you know what I mean."

Miss Tina had never been to Southwest Virginia, and did not know what they meant. She thought that it was a human joke, so she settled under his seat and thought that it might be fun to help him with a little math.

The teacher put problems on the board with chalk and requested the boys to raise their hands. They were supposed to be called by the teacher and give the correct answer. The boy sitting above Miss Tina relied on his fingers to calculate; therefore, he was always last to have his hand raised, and missed earning points and privileges.

Miss Tina loved school and was good at figuring how many mice were running around the field, or how many times she could swat a mouse to sedate it without killing it. So when the teacher pointed to the blackboard with her ruler and tapped five plus five, it was easy for Miss Tina to use one paw to count five and her other paw to count another five. She then tapped with her right paw under the boy's seat ten times! He counted the taps and instantly became a bright and willing student. His classmates, who had once ridiculed him, looked up to him, and he enjoyed his popularity.

Miss Tina continued to attend school and to sit under this special seat until mid-school year. When snow, sleet, and ice fell, she said, "Forget school," and did not show up until the weather broke, much to the student's dismay. He had thought that he was sitting in a magical seat, but when the tapping discontinued his brightness spiraled to failure.

🐾

However, the tapping suddenly returned one warm spring day, much to his delight. Miss Tina had ventured to the campus, anxious to hunt for field mice, loving the warmth of the sun on her winter fur.

The cadets were marching as they did every morning, noon, and night, and Miss Tina got in the rear of the line and marched directly into school, down the hall, and into math class. The teacher on this day was teaching multiplication and said to the class, "Can anyone tell me what two times two is?" Miss Tina, catnapping, dreaming of baby birds, heard the teacher ask this question to her students. Eagerly she tapped four times under the boy's seat. The boy shot his arm into the air and yelled, "Four!" He knew all the answers during math class that day, and as a reward was permitted to go to the library for some free time.

As the student left the classroom, Miss Tina ran swiftly behind and followed him. He was sneaky, and when the correctional officers were chatting, he did not turn to go into the library. The student opened a closet door, walked with Miss Tina at his heels, and shut the door. There was an opening in the ceiling, and he climbed up the wall, shimmied his way through the ceiling, and onto the school's roof. Miss Tina dug her nails into the side of the closet's wall, wiggled her way through the opening, and onto the roof in order to follow.

The student was quick to notice a ladder leaning next to the wall of the school, and he leaned down from the edge of the roof, lowered his body, and shuffled down the ladder. Observantly, Miss Tina thought, *so much for Southwest Virginia mentality!* Once on the ground, he grabbed the ladder and ran to the security fence. He then set the ladder against the security fence, climbed the ladder, and maneuvered the razor wire. Once through the razor wire, he jumped down and was free. Miss Tina remembered seeing the student take off his BDU outfit and run deep into the woods with only boxers, shoes, and socks on. As he left the campus, he pulled down his boxers and mooned the center.

Miss Tina was stuck on the roof, not knowing in which direction to move. She looked over the side of the roof indecisively; the roof was high, and she did not want to jump. By two in the afternoon, the tin roof began to get hot. No shade for comfort, she was beginning to become alarmed at her situation.

Nighttime came and with it brought a thunderstorm with strong winds. Miss Tina had no place to find shelter, and was left to the elements. She scurried along the rooftop, frantically searching for a way down. The trees swayed with each gust of wind, and as the trees swayed, she thought of a way. She thought, *timing is important in life*, and she waited for a strong wind. With a strong wind, a swaying tree limb came over the roof's edge, and with one mighty push from her hindquarters, Miss Tina jumped onto the tree branch and climbed down the tree onto the ground. She scampered home to the flowering-red bush, her place of security, and slept the rest of the night.

# Chapter 8
## Miss Tina's Second Life

Terry always said "A cat has nine lives," and although I did not understand this concept, I witnessed Miss Tina lose one of hers.

January can be a very cold month in Virginia. Sometimes, major snowstorms hit the region, and schools can be closed for a week or more. On this particular Saturday, the pond was covered with ice and a thin layer of snow. As with every Saturday, Terry arrived with her cup of coffee, cell phone in hand, to feed and complete a head count of us. She drove to our feeding station, the red-flowering bush. Although in the month of January, the bush appeared as a twig, it was our feeding station. Terry placed a large wooden-frame doghouse next to the bush, and put straw in our home. This offered us shelter and warmth during the cold winter months.

On this particularly bitter day, Miss Tina was not at the feeding station, and Terry began to call her name. I heard her say, "Tina, Tina," and then I heard the cracking and breaking of ice.

Terry turned to the sound just as Miss Tina broke through the ice. Miss Tina attempted to keep herself afloat. She began to panic and tried to turn herself around. She was in the middle of the pond, and Terry knew that this would mean death to the cat, so she urged Miss Tina to land. Miss Tina continued to struggle, and with each great effort, the ice broke repeatedly. Panic was in Miss Tina's eyes and in the eyes of Terry. Terry unrelentingly called to Miss Tina. She called her in a nonstop manner, urging my baby forward. Time appeared to stand still, and finally Miss Tina came to Terry. She emerged from the icy waters shaking, and stood along the edge and attempted to groom. With the frigid temperature, she was soon shivering, her fur frozen.

Terry took off her coat and covered my baby. She held Miss Tina close to her body. Terry knew that Miss Tina would not be able to survive the coldness, so she put Miss Tina in her car and they left traveling quickly to the emergency veterinarian.

Miss Tina never came back to the center. She went home with Terry once the veterinarian released her.

When Terry returned to the feeding station and was petting me, she told me that Miss Tina deserved to live at her house; my baby had used one of her lives. Terry said that Miss Tina was worthy of the life of luxury, with lots of food and a warm bed. Miss Tina would never be cold again.

# Chapter 9
## The Famous Mister Ed

As Mister Ed developed, he lived up to his name. He was headstrong and opinionated, and occasionally in the wrong place at the wrong time.

I remember the warm summer day when he was catnapping in a golf cart, and one of the boys decided to steal the golf cart and take it on a joyride. The boy, a sixteen-year-old with large buttocks, shoved Mister Ed over, whereupon he had to grip the edge of the seat not to fall out. The boy cranked the engine, and proceeded to drive the golf cart around campus with correctional officers chasing him. He darted around trees, then changed directions and aimed the cart at the officers. An on-call psychologist was summoned to campus in an attempt to discuss feelings, actions, and consequences, but to no avail. The boy laughed, grinned, and aimed the cart at the psychologist, who was seen trying to climb the razorwire fence to get out of the way.

Officers continued running after, and away from the cart. The entire time, the boy had a devious sparkle in his eyes, and Mister Ed continued to appear frozen in time. The golf cart almost overturned a few times during this spree. For most of the ride, Mister Ed feared for his life, as he was seen gripping the dashboard with his front paws. His teeth were clenched, and the whites of his eyes were showing. As I watched this scenario unfolding, I prayed for my son's safety.

🐾

With the breeze blowing in their faces, the boy and Mister Ed drove around campus in the golf cart until it ran out of gas. When the golf cart stopped, the boy was escorted to security, and charged with threatening the security of the institution. He would not be outside playing for a few weeks.

Mister Ed scrambled out of the cart. He was out of breath and collapsed under the red-flowering bush upon his return. Once he gathered his wits, he found his bravado and proceeded to tell his tale. Since I had witnessed the goings-on, I wanted to hear what my son would say to all who were willing to listen.

Mister Ed told his siblings that he had been catnapping on the seat of the cart when he had gotten a brainstorm. He decided to drive the cart to the nearby dump in order to flirt with pussycats. Mister Ed said that he traveled to the dump, and had flirted with about five women. While he told this story, I noted that Julian was mesmerized by this rendition, as he held his mouth open and was drooling. Julian always had an inkling for less wholesome felines, something that would get him into trouble in later years.

When I confronted my son for his misrepresentation, he ignored me and sauntered off into the woods. So much for a good parental talk. As I raised my teenagers, I had to remind myself continually that the frontal lobes of their brains don't mature for about ten years; therefore my adolescent children lacked impulse control and judgment.

## Chapter 10
## The Cat's Out of the Bag

Terry once said, "Humans sometimes come out of closets," although I never really understood what she meant by this saying. She also had another favorite cliché, "The cat's out of the bag!" She said it meant, "Someone spilled the beans." This really confused me; I never saw any beans spilled or a cat coming out of a bag. Sometimes humans have confusing aphorisms, and at times, I am perplexed by the meaning of human words. But for the most part, when I look at a human, I usually know when to meow and when to get out of the way.

I think that the adage is perceived as gossip, and can be damaging to a human's reputation.

Take, for instance, the time when two correctional officers were in the administration building on a fifteen minute break. I once sat on the windowsill at the administration building and watched as two officers were sitting on a couch in front of the fish aquarium. In the first place, I was always interested in this aquarium, as the fish in it were called "convicts." The fish were black with white stripes. I loved watching the convicts swim around, fighting with each other and sometimes eating one another. There was always a power struggle going on in the center's aquarium, and of course, within the correctional center between administrators, officers, nursing staff, and educators.

🐾

As the story goes, two officers requested a smoke break and left their posts to enter the administration building whereupon they planted themselves on the couch and proceeded to become quite playful. They smiled, laughed, and smooched. They reminded me of Charlie Brown and his jest for female felines. With break time over, the two officers did not return to their posts. The lieutenant called for them over the radio. The lieutenant, easily frustrated and angered by their lack of response, sent a sergeant over to the administration building. The happy couple did not hear the door to the administration building open.

Curious by nature and alert to breaking news at the center, I followed the sergeant into the building and witnessed the "cat's out of the bag!" The happy couple took several seconds to become oriented to time and place. The sergeant held his finger on the radio's button so that the entire campus heard him reprimanding the happy couple.

When Terry returned to work the following morning and was reviewing the nighttime log, she shifted in her chair, threw back her head and said, "Oh my, the cat's out of the bag!"

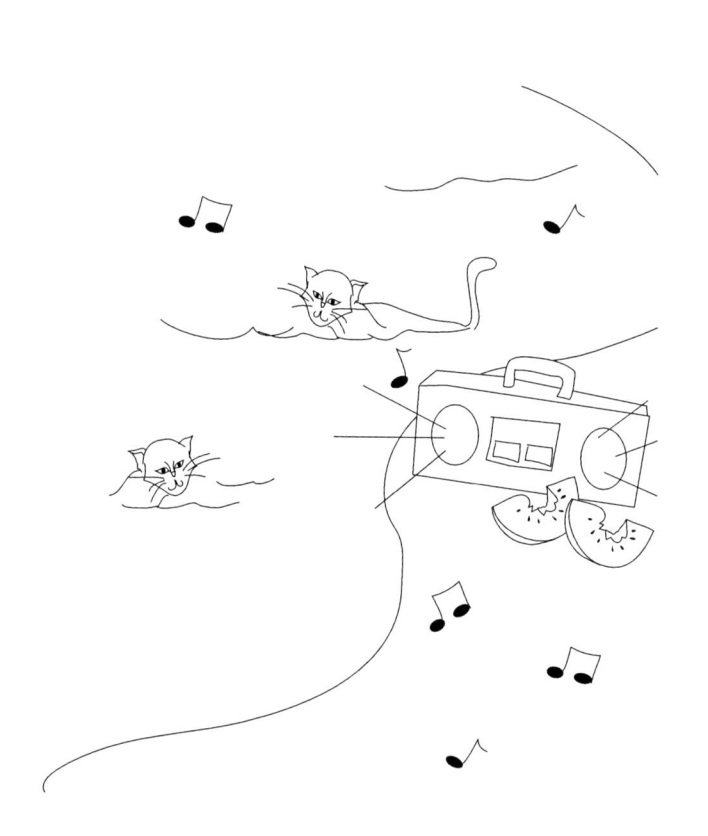

## Chapter 11
## The Dog Days of Summer

When I think about it, a dog really has it better than a feral cat. They get the days of summer named after them. What exactly is a dog day of summer? Does it mean that a dog day is spent in sweltering heat? Or does it mean that during the heat of the summer, a dog spends his day sleeping in a cool spot during the hottest part of the day?

Whatever. Why couldn't the saying be "the cat days of summer?" These are the days in August when cats spend their days trying to stay cool. We lay spread out on moist ground, under trees, or on a dirt floor of a barn or abandoned building. Even a mouse scurrying does not cause us to move; the heat has driven us to ditch the need to hunt and play.

A dog day for Sally was to plant herself inside the air-conditioned administration building in the office of the superintendent. She would lie in front of the air conditioner and would sleep the day away.

The boys especially loved "the dog days of summer," for they enjoyed the pool and played basketball. Often the correctional officers would get into the dog days by planning cookouts, which included lots of watermelon. Sally especially loved to eat watermelon, although it made her pee a lot around campus, much to the consternation of the boys, who sometimes walked barefooted.

🐾

We partied hard once the sun went down. Sally would stroll over to the pool to swim, and my children and I loved to join her. We would all jump into the pool and doggy paddle around, enjoying the coolness of the water and the sound of music from one of the boy's boom boxes. In the distance, fireworks from King's Dominion Theme Park would light the sky.

Sally especially loved to dance, and was always searching for a partner. She treasured the songs by Elvis Presley, "Jail House Rock," and "You Ain't Nothin' but a Hound Dog," and would solicit Julian or Mister Ed to jitterbug with her. The couple would stand erect and strut their stuff. Fur would fly and tails would wag. When Mister Ed danced with Sally, he would grind his hips to the beat and thrash his tail about.

When "You Ain't Nothin' but a Hound Dog," was sung, Sally would attempt to sing along, throwing her face up into the air and howling. With Julian as her partner, he would get his chicken legs moving to the rhythm. One time, he swung her so quickly that he lost her paw and she jitterbugged into the pool!

These fond memories of family life are warm memories placed within my heart. Although living as a feral and having to beg for food at times was no picnic, living at the center and spending the "dog days of summer" with my children will never be forgotten. I can even say that I loved Sally, even though she was a dog.

# Chapter 12
## My Cat's Meow

Throughout my kitten-bearing years, each of my children had special traits and qualities that made them unique. I must have parented forty babies in my heyday, and looking back on my youth, I had a few favorites. I hold my son, Pumpkin Face, extremely close to my heart.

From the beginning of his life, he was a thoughtful cat, and chose to stay close to me. As a black and white longhaired cat with a triangular mark on his face, he reminded Terry of a jack-o'-lantern. She would say that he had a "silly cat face," a face only Terry and I could love.

Pumpkin Face enjoyed the center, and especially loved to prowl the cattle farm. He cherished a snooze in the warm sun near the cattle, and appreciated the barn as he idled his time away, waiting for field mice to come into the barn to munch on some feed. When he caught a mouse, Pumpkin would proudly prance home and surprise me with his find. Many a time, I would praise him, and then let the mouse scurry off into the field.

One of my son's favorite pastimes was to watch the fish in the aquarium. The fish, or convicts, were aggressive at times, especially during mating season. After babies were born, it was normal to see them swimming at a frantic pace, nipping at one another and, at times, reverting to cannibalism.

Pumpkin would sneak into the administration building when the basement door was opened, and walk up the stairs into the lobby to spend his afternoon watching and planning how to capture a convict. At times, Sally would see him and chase him back to the basement, as she did not want to give up her spot with the superintendent. She loved his office and the doggie treats that he gave her daily.

One day, Pumpkin set out to catch a convict. He crept up the basement steps and methodically slithered over the carpet, not making a sound. As luck would have it, the top portion of the aquarium was off, as my human friend, Tina, was cleaning the tank. While Tina was not looking, Pumpkin took a quick swipe with his left paw and clutched the squirming fish. He sprinted down the steps, out of the basement, and to the red-flowering bush.

Pumpkin presented me with his catch of the day, and we enjoyed the delicacy of eating a convict. I had never seen him so proud of his accomplishment. On that day and forever more, he was indeed my cat's meow.

# Chapter 13
## Barking Up the Wrong Tree

Mister Ed loved to roam the campus and tease the boys. He would watch the boys playing football, and when one of them grew tired and sat on top of the picnic table, he would creep over and jump quickly onto the boy's leg, attaching himself. The boy would grimace in pain from Mister Ed's sharp nails. Mister Ed would then run up the nearest tree, staying on a branch until the correctional officers summoned the boys back to their cottages.

On that crisp fall day, with a slight breeze from the north, some of the colorful leaves had fallen to the ground. The leaves were swirling in circles in various spots around campus. That was the first sweater day of the fall season and the boys were playing football.

Mister Ed was waiting for his moment to pounce on a boy, when there was a commotion outside of the dining hall. He didn't bother to look, but took the timing of this tumult to strike and escape up the nearest tree, just as one of the boys ran from the dining hall and climbed up the same tree.

With both cat and boy in the tree, the correctional officers were alerted that an inmate attempted to go AWOL. Officers surrounded the tree with their radios blaring, attempting to entice the boy down from the tree with food, which attracted Mister Ed, who was always hungry.

🐾

Mister Ed always had some greediness to him, and being up in the tree with the boy brought out the worst of his bad-tempered personality. He wanted to come down from the tree to feast on roast and gravy-mashed potatoes. So he hissed at the officers in an attempt to get them to flee.

After one hour transpired, the officers were getting stiff-necked and angry, so they decided to try to shake the inmate out of the tree. Mister Ed clung to a branch, not willing to fall. Sally heard the uproar and decided to join in the fun. She came bounding onto campus and stood with the officers, barking at the tree with her tail wagging. At one point, she yowled and pointed with one foot and her tail standing straight. It was apparent to all that the hunter had come out in Sally. She particularly enjoyed all the food at the base of the tree, much to the dismay of Mister Ed who wanted to gouge her eyes out.

As nighttime descended onto campus, spotlights were turned on and a helicopter circled overhead. The Secretary of the Department of Public Safety was contacted and apprised of the situation. He demanded action. The idea of using a chain saw was suggested.

The boy, at times, would shimmy along branches, trying to reach Mister Ed. His intent was to grab the cat and throw him onto the officers. As he crawled along the branches and almost touched Mister Ed, he could be heard saying, "It's better you than me, baby."

At last, the plan was for the officers to chop down the tree. They were weary from standing under the tree, and their shift was ending. Sally had grown tired of the sport and had returned to the maintenance building where she had her bed and food. She squatted at the base of the tree leaving her mark, much to the repulsion of the officers.

With the first thrust of the chain saw into the trunk of the tree, Mister Ed decided to jump. When he did, he landed on the baldhead of the lieutenant in charge of security, who was brandishing the chain saw. With the cat on his head, the lieutenant fell to the ground. The chain saw flew through the air, landing on the branch where the inmate was sitting. The boy confiscated the chain saw, jumped down the tree, and chased the lieutenant around campus. The correctional officers scattered.

The boy grew tired of this sport and gave up after about twenty minutes. As he turned the chain saw off and handed it to an officer, he could be heard laughing. The boy was escorted to the maximum-security cottage.

Mister Ed returned to the feeding station fatigued. He did not boast of this event, but went directly to bed without eating his supper. Late into the evening, he could be heard talking in his sleep, saying, "There's no place like home."

## Chapter 14
### Momma's New Home

The trap-neuter-return program was successful. Many cats were placed for adoption and left the center to live in a home with humans. Try as she might, Terry was unable to get me to walk into a trap so that I could be neutered. Much to her dismay, I continued to have litter after litter, until Terry's last day of work.

Terry was determined to catch me and take me to her home. She did not want to leave me at the center because she had a strong attachment to me. I loved to follow her around, as we had become friends.

Terry and Tina devised a plan, and Terry opened the door to the foyer of the administration building. They cornered me; Tina picked me up by my scruff, and placed me in a cat carrier.

I became an indoor cat, a pivotal moment in my life. What a wonderful existence. No more wet, cold, or dog days of summer. I was introduced to other family members, and became reacquainted with my daughter, Miss Tina. Terry's canary, Sunny Boy, and her oversized guinea pig, Max, intrigued me. It seemed odd to have all of these animals in one little house.

While Terry was at work, I loved spending the day watching Sunny Boy jump from one perch to another. He was very tempting. Terry was smart enough to have

Sunny's cage hanging from the ceiling near a window, so that the bird could have a view of the outdoors. At times, Miss Tina would climb onto the windowsill and jump. She would land on top of the birdcage where she would remain for a few seconds. During these few seconds, the poor bird would stop singing and breathe rapidly. Miss Tina played this game throughout the day. Terry never knew what we did when she was not at home. She told her friends that she had noticed Sunny losing some feathers, and he had developed a "nervous tic."

Max, the guinea pig, came out of his cage twice a day when Terry cleaned and fed him. She loved to hold Max and tell him how handsome he was. I thought he was handsome too, but for a different reason. I had never seen such a large, fat, soft rodent! Max was given treats daily. He loved lettuce, carrots, and apples. Terry loved Max, and I couldn't help but think how wonderful it would be to catch and eat him. The fat on this rodent fascinated me, especially his chin, where there were layers and layers of soft fatdraping onto the floor.

All of us coexisted, and although we were not "the farmer in the dell," we did enjoy entertaining each other while Terry was away. I especially enjoyed spending time sunbathing by the window. While lying by the window, I was able to look over Terry's farmland. I was able to see horses, dogs, and birds. Squirrels were around, eating with the birds. At times, I witnessed feral cats venturing onto the farm where they spent part of the day near bird feeders.

Terry neutered two tabby-type cats that decided to make the farm their residence. She had a feeding station for them in her barn, and spent time with these cats as she did with me when I had lived at the center. She named one tabby Pretty Kitty, and the other Scare-de-Cat.

Terry told me that she would care for these two cats until death, as a feral cat typically does not live long, only about five years. Terry said that a feral cat has a difficult life and that if humans would take responsibility of their pets, this problem would not exist. I guess that I was a lucky feral, now that I have a home and Terry to take care of me.

# Chapter 15
## The Empty Cat Syndrome

As with any mother, I missed my offspring when I left the center. However, Miss Tina was with me at my new home. Terry kept me posted as to how my adult children were doing as she continued to volunteer to feed and to take care of the cats. Her mission was to have the feral cats adopted, and those that were not adoptable would be neutered and returned to the center.

My children were no longer teenagers, but were adults, able to care for themselves and to make decisions. Some of them made sound decisions, while others were reckless. Some lived lives that caused me to worry and be concerned.

Three of my children, with Charlie Brown's traits, ended up in unhappy situations. Julian, who was always attempting to please Ms. Heavens, ran from the center one night after an argument with her. He took up residence at the nearby dump and started to live with a female non-neutered dump cat. Julian was too proud to return to the center, and was last seen foraging for food at the landfill. This situation reminded me of a song that I heard by Confederate Railroad while listening to a country station.

> *"Yeah, an' I like my women just a little*
> *on the trashy side.*

❖

*When they wear their clothes too tight
and their hair is dyed
Too much lipstick an' too much rouge,
Gets me excited, leaves me feeling
confused.
An' I like my women just a little on the
trashy side."*

Ms. Heavens drowned shortly after Julian left. Always self-absorbed and in search of some afternoon delight, she planned a fishing trip. She drowned in her quest for tuna.

Mister Ed left the center on one of his adventures. He was last seen at the Pamunkey Regional Jail, serving time. The inmates, as part of their rehabilitation, were permitted to own a cat. Mister Ed is owned by one of the inmates. He is cooped up in a small cell and is ordered around, much to his displeasure. He cowers when his owner comes looking for him, and has not seen the outside of his jail cell since confinement.

My adventurous boy, Midnight, came home with Terry one evening after hurting his knee. Terry said that since Midnight was unable to run quickly, he wouldn't be able to defend himself. She said that he needed to live a carefree life in a safe and loving environment. I was so happy to see Midnight and to have him near.

## Chapter 16
## Pumpkin's Ninth Life

I think that some felines go through their nine lives at a faster rate, using them in rapid succession. Others take each of their lives and spend years within one, stopping to smell the roses along the way, so to speak.

The saying "life isn't fair" plays repeatedly in my head; I think the saying is true about my son, Pumpkin Face.

The political climate at the center had a drastic shift when superintendents were transferred and Donald left Hanover. The new superintendent loved dogs and listened to the negativism of the staff that did not like us. We were blamed for scratching cars, and when a family of raccoons set up residence on campus, we were blamed for attracting raccoons.

My favorite son, Pumpkin, did not come to Terry's for many years. He loved the center, and as long as volunteers fed and petted him, he was content.

However, when the political climate changed, cats were trapped and sent off to the pound. Hanover cats were not adopted at the pound, and were destroyed.

Pumpkin Face eluded the traps and was never caught. When he became the lone surviving cat of the center, the superintendent directed staff to stop feeding him. He would cry for his food on the administration steps, only to be ignored. Staff feared losing their jobs if they fed Pumpkin. He cried daily for food.

Upon hearing of this situation, Terry, who had been banned from the center, sneaked onto the property with a cat carrier in hand, determined to locate Pumpkin. When Terry called for Pumpkin, he ran from the woods. She held him, kissed him, and placed him lovingly in the cat carrier.

Pumpkin began his ninth life at Terry's horse farm. I loved to watch him from the windows. He made friends with the two tabbies, Pretty Kitty and Scare-de-Cat, and especially loved the horses and bird-watching.

Pumpkin had his very own feeding station where I could view him from Terry's bedroom window. He loved to sun himself on top of an old wooden table where she placed his food. He was comfortable at the horse farm, and loved his best friend Terry, who would spend time feeding, petting, and talking to him daily. Pumpkin especially loved his new cathouse, and treasured his house, which was the same cathouse he had lived in at the center. He could smell his friends, although he never knew what had happened to them.

One evening, when Terry returned from work, she noticed that Pumpkin was sneezing. She quickly took him to the veterinarian where he was treated for a cold. Terry thought that Pumpkin would be fine, but when she went to his feeding station the next morning, he had died on top of his feeding table, waiting for Terry.

On that hot July morning, I looked from Terry's bedroom window, and I heard Terry crying. It was more than crying, Terry was sobbing and petting my Pumpkin Face.

🐾

I noticed Terry digging a hole. This took a long time because she stopped every several shovels to pet Pumpkin. After she finished digging the hole, she stood looking at it. Tears dripped into the hole, moistening the dirt. I could hear Terry speaking to my son. She gently picked him up from the table and placed him lovingly in his hole. I watched as she placed his favorite gray mouse with him.

As she threw shovels of dirt covering Pumpkin, I heard her say a children's rhyme.

> *"The little cares*
> *that fretted me,*
> *I lost them yesterday*
> *Among the fields*
> *above the sea,*
> *Among the winds at play."*

Terry stood over Pumpkin's grave. She slid his cathouse over his grave and placed flowers inside of his house. As she cried, she petted the two tabbies that had wandered from the barn to be with her. She held and kissed them. Terry lovingly placed the tabbies on Pumpkin's table and said good-bye.

# Epilogue

The Virginia Department of Juvenile Justice has not taken responsibility for the destruction of a neutered colony of cats that resided at Hanover Juvenile Correctional Center from 1997 to 2004. The colony of six to eight cats was trapped and taken to Hanover County's local pound, where they were destroyed, as well as raccoons and other wildlife that happened upon the traps.

The Departments of Juvenile Justice and Public Safety received e-mails from concerned citizens about the situation. Articles were published about the senseless destruction of wildlife at the juvenile center in local newspapers, and members of Hanover Humane were instrumental in getting the word out to Virginians about what had transpired at the center.

However, the Department of Juvenile Justice and the Department of Public Safety minimized what was revealed. Citizens were left to believe that the cats were at the animal pound, and that wildlife had been set free in a "remote" area of Hanover County.

The Department of Juvenile Justice intentionally misled the public and has not taken ownership for this annihilation. Since Hanover Juvenile Correctional Center is located in a rural area, feral cats and wildlife will return, it is only a matter of time.

Miss Tina, Midnight, and Momma Mola reside with the author. They left the center prior to the superintendent's destructive actions. Pumpkin Face was the lone surviving cat of this carnage having escaped trapping. He was successfully removed from the facility and transitioned to the author's horse farm. Pumpkin Face died from an upper respiratory infection on July 19, 2005.

**"Truth stands the test of time;
Lies are soon exposed."
Proverbs 12:19**

# Bibliography

Walley, Dean. <u>The Little Book of Proverbs</u>. Kansas City: Hallmark, 1968.